About the Author

MARK TWAIN, who was born Samuel L. Clemens in Missouri in 1835, wrote some of the most enduring works of literature in the English language, including *The Adventures of Tom Sawyer* and *The Adventures of Huckleberry Finn*. He died in 1910.

The WAR PRAYER

The WAR PRAYER

Mark Twain

with drawings by JOHN GROTH

Perennial

An Imprint of HarperCollins*Publishers*

A hardcover edition of this book was published in 1968 by St. Crispin Press, in association with Harper & Row, Publishers, Inc.

THE WAR PRAYER. Copyright © 1923, 1951 by The Mark Twain Company. Drawings copyright © 1968 by John Groth. All rights reserved. Printed in the United States of America. No part of this book may be used or reproduced in any manner whatsoever without written permission except in the case of brief quotations embodied in critical articles and reviews. For information address HarperCollins Publishers Inc., 10 East 53rd Street, New York, NY 10022.

HarperCollins books may be purchased for educational, business, or sales promotional use. For information please write: Special Markets Department, HarperCollins Publishers Inc., 10 East 53rd Street, New York, NY 10022.

First Harper paperback edition published 1970.

Reissued in Perennial 2002.

Library of Congress Cataloging-in-Publication Data

Twain, Mark, 1835-1910.
   The war prayer.

   (Harper colophon books)
   Originally published in 1923 as part of the author's Europe and elsewhere.
   I. Title
PS1322.W3 1984   813'.4   83-49018
ISBN 0-06-091113-1 (pbk.)

02 03 04 05 06   20 19 18 17 16 15

To Dan Beard, who dropped in to see him,
Clemens read the "War Prayer," stating that
he had read it to his daughter Jean,
and others, who had told him he must not
print it, for it would be regarded as sacrilege.

"Still, you are going to publish it, are you not?"

Clemens, pacing up and down the room
in his dressing-gown and slippers,
shook his head.

"No," he said, "I have told the whole truth
in that, and only dead men can tell the truth
in this world.

"It can be published after I am dead."

Mark Twain, A Biography by Albert Bigelow Paine
Harper & Brothers, 1912

The WAR PRAYER

It was a time of great and
exalting excitement.

The country was up in arms,
the war was on,
in every breast
burned the holy fire of patriotism;
the drums were beating,
the bands playing,
the toy pistols popping,
the bunched firecrackers
hissing and spluttering;
on every hand and far down
the receding and fading spread
of roofs and balconies
a fluttering wilderness of flags
flashed in the sun;
daily the young volunteers marched
down the wide avenue

gay and fine in their new uniforms,
the proud fathers and mothers
and sisters and sweethearts
cheering them with voices
choked with happy emotion
as they swung by;
nightly the packed mass meetings
listened, panting, to patriot oratory
which stirred the deepest deeps
of their hearts
and which they interrupted
at briefest intervals
with cyclones of applause,
the tears running down their cheeks
the while;
in the churches the pastors preached
devotion to flag and country
and invoked the God of Battles,
beseeching His aid in our good cause

in outpouring of fervid eloquence
which moved every listener.
It was indeed a glad and gracious time,
and the half-dozen rash spirits
that ventured to disapprove of the war
and cast a doubt upon its righteousness
straightway got such a stern
and angry warning
that for their personal safety's sake
they quickly shrank out of sight
and offended no more in that way.

Sunday morning came—
next day the battalions would leave
for the front;
the church was filled;
the volunteers were there,
their young faces
alight with martial dreams—

visions of the stern advance,

the gathering momentum,

the rushing charge, the flashing sabers,

the flight of the foe, the tumult,

the enveloping smoke, the fierce pursuit,

the surrender!—

then home from the war,

bronzed heroes, welcomed, adored,

submerged in golden seas of glory!

With the volunteers sat their dear ones,

proud, happy, and envied

by the neighbors and friends

who had no sons and brothers

to send forth to the field of honor,

there to win for the flag or failing,

die the noblest of noble deaths.

The service proceeded; a war chapter

from the Old Testament was read;

the first prayer was said;

it was followed by an organ burst
that shook the building,
and with one impulse the house rose,
with glowing eyes and beating hearts,
and poured out
that tremendous invocation—

God the all-terrible!
Thou who ordainest,
Thunder thy clarion
and lightning thy sword!

Then came the "long" prayer.
None could remember the like of it
for passionate pleading
and moving and beautiful language.
The burden of its supplication was
that an ever-merciful and benignant
Father of us all would watch over
our noble young soldiers

and aid, comfort, and encourage them
in their patriotic work;
bless them, shield them in the day
of battle and the hour of peril,
bear them in His mighty hand,
make them strong and confident,
invincible in the bloody onset;
help them to crush the foe,
grant to them
and to their flag and country
imperishable honor and glory—

An aged stranger entered and moved
with slow and noiseless step
up the main aisle,
his eyes fixed upon the minister,
his long body clothed in a robe
that reached to his feet, his head bare,
his white hair descending

in a frothy cataract to his shoulders,
his seamy face unnaturally pale,
pale even to ghastliness.
With all eyes following him
and wondering,
he made his silent way;
without pausing, he ascended
to the preacher's side
and stood there, waiting.
With shut lids the preacher,
unconscious of his presence,
continued his moving prayer,
and at last finished it with the words,
uttered in fervent appeal,
"Bless our arms,
grant us the victory,
O Lord our God,
Father and Protector
of our land and flag!"

The stranger touched his arm,
motioned him to step aside—
which the startled minister did—
and took his place.
During some moments
he surveyed the spellbound audience
with solemn eyes in which burned
an uncanny light;
then in a deep voice he said:

"I come from the Throne—
bearing a message from Almighty God!"
The words smote the house with a shock;
if the stranger perceived it
he gave no attention.
"He has heard the prayer
of His servant your shepherd
and will grant it
if such shall be your desire

after I, His messenger,
shall have explained to you its import—
that is to say, its full import.
For it is like unto
many of the prayers of men,
in that it asks for more
than he who utters it is aware of—
except he pause and think.

"God's servant and yours
has prayed his prayer.
Has he paused and taken thought?
Is it one prayer?
No, it is two—
one uttered, the other not.
Both have reached the ear
of Him Who heareth all supplications,
the spoken and the unspoken.
Ponder this—keep it in mind.

If you would beseech
a blessing upon yourself, beware!
lest without intent
you invoke a curse upon a neighbor
at the same time.
If you pray for the blessing of rain
upon your crop which needs it,
by that act you are possibly praying
for a curse upon some neighbor's crop
which may not need rain
and can be injured by it.

"You have heard your servant's prayer—
the uttered part of it.
I am commissioned of God
to put into words the other part of it—
that part which the pastor,
and also you in your hearts,
fervently prayed silently.

And ignorantly and unthinkingly?
God grant that it was so!
You heard these words:
'Grant us the victory,
O Lord our God!'
That is sufficient.
The *whole* of the uttered prayer
is compact into those pregnant words.
Elaborations were not necessary.
When you have prayed for victory
you have prayed for
many unmentioned results
which follow victory—*must* follow it,
cannot help but follow it.
Upon the listening spirit
of God the Father fell also
the unspoken part of the prayer.
He commandeth me
to put it into words.

LISTEN!

"O Lord our Father,

our young patriots,
idols of our hearts,
go forth to battle—
be Thou near them!

With them, in spirit,
we also go forth
from the sweet peace
of our beloved firesides
to smite the foe.

O Lord our God,

help us
to tear their soldiers
to bloody shreds
with our shells;

help us
to cover their smiling fields
with the pale forms
of their patriot dead;

help us
to drown the thunder
of the guns
with the shrieks
of their wounded,
writhing in pain;

help us
to lay waste
their humble homes
with a hurricane of fire;

help us
to wring the hearts
of their unoffending widows
with unavailing grief;

help us
to turn them out roofless
with their little children
to wander unfriended
the wastes
of their desolated land

in rags and hunger
and thirst,
sports of the sun flames
of summer
and the icy winds
of winter,

broken in spirit,

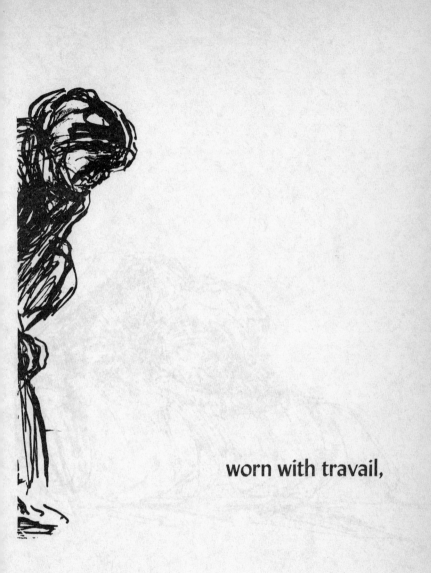

worn with travail,

imploring Thee
for the refuge of the grave
and denied it—

for our sakes
who adore Thee, Lord,

blast their hopes,

blight their lives,

protract their bitter pilgrimage,

make heavy their steps,

water their way with their tears,

stain the white snow
with the blood
of their wounded feet!

We ask it,
in the spirit of love,
of Him Who is the Source of Love,

and Who is the ever-faithful
refuge and friend
of all that are sore beset

**and seek His aid
with humble and contrite hearts.**

AMEN.

After a pause:

"Ye have prayed it;
   if ye still desire it,
   speak!
The messenger of the
   Most High waits."

It was believed afterward
that the man was a lunatic,
because there was no sense
in what he said.